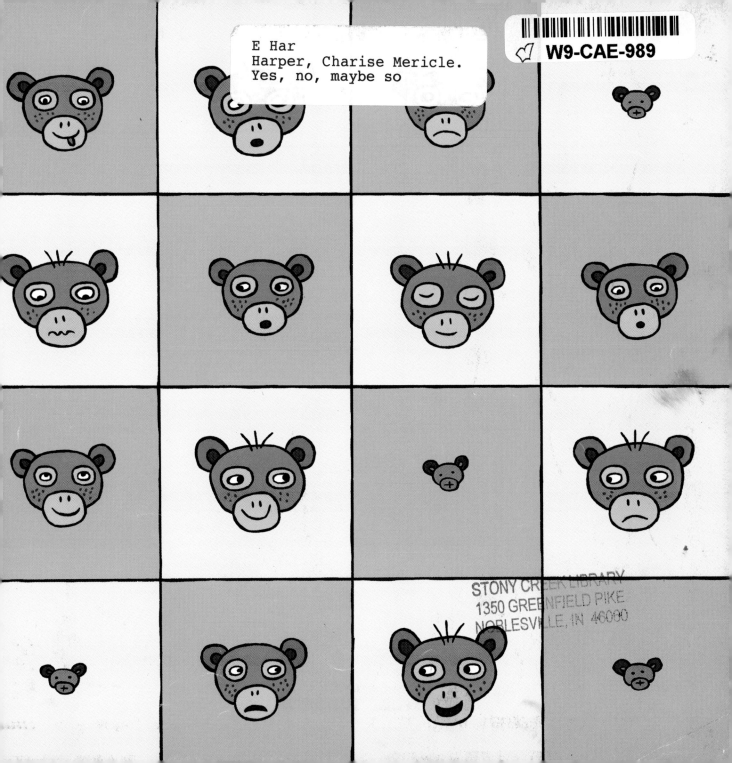

For one little brother Carter and one big brother Justin.
Fill your days with Maybe So's.

Published by Dial Books for Young Readers
A division of Penguin Young Readers Group
345 Hudson Street • New York, New York 10014
Copyright © 2004 by Charise Mericle Harper
All rights reserved
Designed by Kimi Weart • Text set in New Century Schoolbook
Manufactured in China on acid-free paper
10 9 8 7 6 5 4 3 2 1

LIBRARY OF CONGRESS CATALOGING-IN-PUBLICATION DATA
Harper, Charise Mericle.
Yes, no, maybe so / by Charise Mericle Harper.
    p.   cm.
Summary: Two little monkey brothers go through a day of actions that are yes
(appropriate), no (inappropriate), or maybe so (possible?).
ISBN 0-8037-2956-1
[1. Monkeys—Fiction. 2. Brothers—Fiction. 3. Behavior—Fiction.] I. Title.
PZ7.H231323Ye 2004   [E]—dc22   2003012836

The art is hand-drawn line art colored in Photoshop.

BOUNCE

YES

Bouncy me!

Bouncy brother?

Bounce with brother?

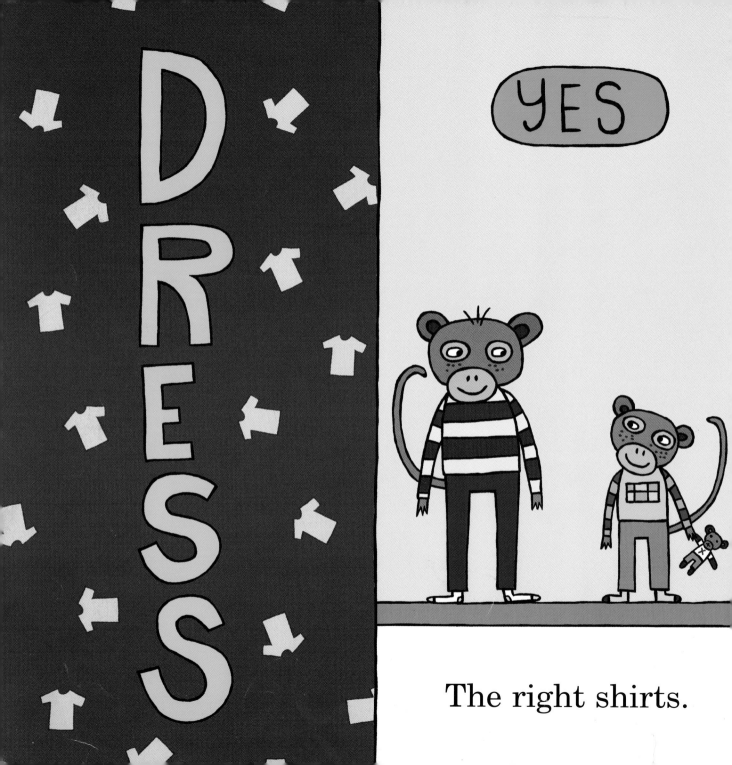

The right shirts.

The wrong pants.

Sharing socks?

EAT

YES

Just right.

Too tippy! | A perfect fort?

RIDE

YES

Up we go.

Oh, no!

Whee!

Way up high.

Not each other.   Into leaves!

PICNIC

YES

With Teddy.

Warm sand castles.

No wiggly worms! | Splashy puddles?

Not from a fishbowl.   From a sprinkler?

SHARE

YES

From one bowl.

Not by throwing.   Trading bites?

READ

YES

Right side up.

Not upside down.   Why not?

With bubbles!

Not with clothes. With swimsuits?

Good night.

Too crowded.   Just right.

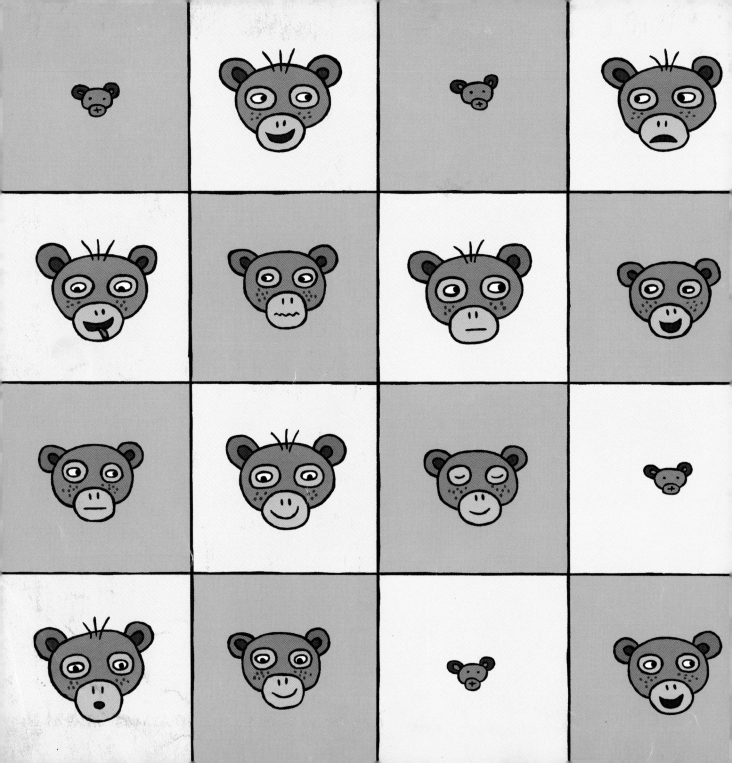